Auld Lang Syne

Auld Lang Syne

by Joanne Findon
paintings by Ted Nasmith

Stoddart Kids

*We acknowledge the Canada Council for the Arts and the
Ontario Arts Council for their support of our publishing program.*

Published in Canada in 1997 by Stoddart Kids,
a division of Stoddart Publishing Co. Limited
34 Lesmill Road
Toronto, Canada M3B 2T6
Tel (416) 445-3333 FAX (416) 445-5967
e-mail Customer.Service@ccmailgw.genpub.com

Published in the United States in 1998 by Stoddart Kids
85 River Rock Drive, Suite 202
Buffalo, New York 14207
Toll free 1-800-805-1083
e-mail gdsinc@genpub.com

Canadian Cataloguing in Publication Data

Findon, Joanne, 1957-
Auld lang syne

ISBN 0-7737-3006-0

1. Burns, robert, 1759-1796 — Biography — Juvenile literature.
2. Poets, Scottish — 18th century — Biography — Juvenile literature.
I. Nasmith, Ted.   II. Title.

PR4331.F56 1997   j821'.6   C97-930626-4

Printed and bound in Hong Kong, China by
Book Art Inc., Toronto

For Charlene, Cordelia, Debi, Evelyn, and Tina,
my old friends.
—J.F.

To my sister Cathy and my Aunt Joy,
the unofficial guardians of the family archives;
to James Dunbar Nasmith of Edinburgh;
and to my children.
—T.N.

Robert Burns
portrait by Alexander Nasmyth
with permission of The Scottish National Portrait Gallery

Introduction

Robert Burns was born in southern Scotland in 1759. Although his father was a poor farmer, Robert grew up in a house filled with songs, stories and love.

Childhood poverty left him with broken health, but by the time of Burns' death in 1796, his poems and rewritten versions of old Scottish songs had made him famous.

Two hundred years after his death, Robert Burns is still one of the best-loved poets in the world. Lines from his many works are known and often quoted, but one song in particular is so familiar that it is a tradition to sing it, especially on New Year's Eve. Wherever people gather to reflect on the passage of time, or to celebrate the joys of friendship, home and family, it is not unusual for them to "take a cup of kindness yet, for *Auld Lang Syne*".

On the day of my birth, Father was riding to the town of Ayr to fetch an attendant for my mother when he met an old gypsy woman. The weather was stormy, and a swollen stream had burst over the road blocking her way. The woman begged him to carry her across. Despite his haste, he took the time to do so. Imagine his surprise when he returned from Ayr to find this same woman sitting by the fireside in our cottage! I, the newborn babe, was cradled in her arms. She examined my tiny palm carefully, then uttered a prophecy. Years later, I turned her words into a bit of rhyme:

> *He'll have misfortunes great and small*
> > *But aye a heart above them all.*
> *He'll be a credit to us all:*
> > *We'll all be proud of Robin!*

*F*ather was a poor tenant farmer who toiled all day in the fields. Our food was plain peasant fare: kale and potatoes when we had them, and meat only rarely. Sometimes we had nothing but porridge for our supper. Our cottage was long and low, and had only four small windows. Yet this was a house lit with laughter and song, and the bonds of love meant more to us than wealth.

In the evenings, when the day's work was done, Father would read to us from the Bible or from one of the other books that he kept on the shelf by the fire. When his voice grew weary, Mother would sing us ballads or tell us tales. My mother had a great store of songs and stories that she had learned as a child, and she would entertain us with old country yarns — of ghosts and fairies and witches, of giants and kelpies, of elf-candles and enchanted towers and haunted churchyards — tales that made us shiver and move closer to the winking firelight. To this day I am a wee bit fearful of ghosts and witches, and keep a sharp lookout when I walk abroad at night.

My mother's stories shimmered in my memory as I grew, and years later I made some of them into poems.

*F*ather understood the importance of learning and did his very best to give us an education. Friends who entered our home at the dinner hour often found us all sitting with a book in one hand and a spoon in the other. In my seventh year, Father and several neighbours put what hard-earned money they could spare towards hiring a teacher for us village children.

One golden summer, Father even sent me to study in the town of Ayr. I became friends with several boys there. After a week at lessons, we would spend carefree Sunday afternoons wandering among the burns and braes beyond the town, tracking grasshoppers to their haunts, or watching the minnows frisk in sunny pools. How it grieved me when that summer ended and I had to part with those young lads! Some I never saw again, for like many in our impoverished countryside, they sailed away to seek their fortune and did not return. Whether they found their dreams or even survived the adventure, is something I do not know.

We two have paddled in the burn
From morning sun till dine,
But seas between us broad have roared
Since auld lang syne.

*A*las, that famine-faced spectre, Poverty, was a constant visitor in our home. The soil on our land was poor and we were always in debt. Father moved us to another farm at Lochlie, but it proved to be no better. To make matters worse, we were pursued by a greedy landlord who claimed we owed him money. My blood yet boils at the memory of that scoundrel's threatening letters, which often had us all in tears around the table.

There was no money to hire farm workers, and so from the age of thirteen I laboured in the fields. By evening, when the setting sun would release me from my task, I was often so tired I could barely speak.

*B*ut it was in these hard times that poetry first burned within me. I would rush through my midday meal, then climb up to the attic room and steal a bit of time writing feverishly on my little slate. My heart was constantly ablaze with one passion or another: with rage at our poverty, with love for a neighbour lass, or with pity for the frightened creatures of the field, like the mouse whose nest I turned up with my plough.

*W*hen I was eighteen we moved again to a farm with better soil in the heartland of Kyle. But the bloodhounds of Misfortune pursued us still. Bad weather and failed crops added to our mounting debts. My dear father, worn out from overwork and constant worry, fell ill and died.

What good were my poems in such a world? They could not feed us or keep us warm. They had no power to snatch my father from Death's chill grip. One winter evening my thoughts were running thus, while wretched and alone I sat by the fire.

Click! went the latch. I looked up as the door swung open. There, bathed in the glow of firelight, stood a shining maiden. She wore a lustrous green gown wrought with an intricate pattern of light and shadow. A wreath of holly crowned her head.

"All hail! My own inspired bard!" she sang.

She told me that her name was Coila, and that she had watched me since my birth, listening to my awkward rhymes with hope for the future. She urged me not to abandon my craft, but to serve her by writing of Scotland's joys and sorrows. She bound the wreath of holly around my head, then vanished into the darkness outside.

The vision left me breathless. I lingered by the dying fire, filled with new purpose and a determination to carry on with my poetry.

*T*hat meeting with my Scottish Muse seemed to change my luck as well, for I was soon to meet Jean Armour, the bonnie, dark-haired lass who would become my wife.

I was walking through town one morning with my dog Luath, when I noticed two young women spreading freshly washed linens on the grass to bleach in the sun. The activity caught his eye and off frisked my wee Luath. He was soon leaping rapturously over the white cloths with his muddy feet! One of the girls threw a stone at him and I was immediately fired with indignation. I ran to her, blazing with anger, but her beautiful, flashing eyes stopped me from scolding her as I intended.

"Lassie," I told her, "if ye had any respect for Poet Burns ye would not be throwing stones at his poor wee dog!"

"I have no respect for Poet Burns!" she retorted, and seemed about to throw stones at *me* when she halted and began to laugh at my pained expression.

Thus began our romance. And what anguish we would suffer before we finally found peace! For two years Jean's angry father forbade her marriage to a poor cotter's son. Oh, but what joy it was when we finally set up house together!

Some of my happiest hours were spent with friends in town. It was there that I was encouraged to try to publish my poetry.

Most of my works had been hand copied and passed around among my friends, and although they had met with considerable favour in our country circle, I had not thought them worthy of a larger audience. My friends disagreed. "How can you resist the temptation of sending verses of such merit to the magazines?" was a question I heard more than once. They helped me to find a publisher, and soon my first little book of poems was launched upon the world.

*B*y the time I set out for Edinburgh on a borrowed pony to publish the second edition of my poems, I had achieved a small amount of fame. Nevertheless, I was surprised one evening along the way, when I stopped at the home of a friend, to learn that he had invited all the farmers in the parish for a dinner in my honour! The sign of my arrival was to be a white sheet tied to a pitchfork and placed on top of a corn stack. At this signal, everyone streamed out of their homes and converged on my friend's cottage. Mirth and merriment continued into the wee small hours.

One day I fled the clamour of Edinburgh's streets in the company of another new friend, the painter Alexander Nasmyth. We climbed up to Arthur's Seat, a rocky hill which commands a view of a dozen counties in all directions. Beyond the cramped rows of city houses stretched the countryside with its little dwellings, each one sending up a plume of smoke.

As we stood in the sun admiring the vista, I told Alexander, "The sight of so many smoking cottages reminds me of all the happiness and worth that each one contains." And I knew with great certainty that I would never be at home among the noble families of Edinburgh. My heart would ever dwell among the peasant folk.

> *We two have run about the braes,*
> *And pulled the gowans fine,*
> *But we've wandered many a weary fit*
> *Since auld lang syne.*

Determined to live up to my new title of Scottish Bard and eager for fresh themes to celebrate, I set out on a series of trips through Scotland.

I rode northward into the beautiful Highlands, where I travelled many miles among gloomy, savage glens and cliffs grey with eternal snow.

I became absolutely crazed about finding old verses and tunes that had never been written down before. Some were mere fragments, and I set about writing new words to the music. If I did not recover them, many would be lost forever. There was a peculiar wild happiness in these old songs that cast a spell of enchantment over me.

One of these was "Auld Lang Syne". I wrote it down as an old man sang it for me. Of the words he knew only a few, but they seemed to me to be of such genius that I began to compose more to fill out the song.

Light be the turf on the breast of the heaven-inspired poet who wrote this glorious verse.

> *And there's a hand my trusty fiere,*
> *And give's a hand of thine,*
> *And we'll take a right guid-willie waught,*
> *For auld lang syne.*

*A*lthough my second edition of poems brought me some income, I had not the means to wander Scotland forever. I returned home to my bonnie Jean.

I leased a new farm, but it proved to be no more successful than others from my past. Desperate to feed Jeanie and our five wee bairns, I became a tax collector for the Excise. Tax collectors are called "gaugers" by many folk, and are not popular in the countryside. Still, I enjoy the work for I can compose verses as I ride along.

I have been frequently ill of late, but even so, I have been able to continue work on the old Scottish songs that mean so much to me. I have just sent the latest set to my friend and publisher James Johnson. Among them is my favourite, "Auld Lang Syne".

It captures more than any other the joys of friendship, the sorrow of partings, and the ever-fervent hope of future meetings. I hope it will find a special place in my readers' hearts as well. May we meet again.

Should auld acquaintance be forgot,
And never brought to mind?
Should auld acquaintance be forgot,
And days of auld lang syne?

Glossary

auld lang syne	literally "old long since"; good old times
aye	ever
bairns	children
bard	a poet, especially a national poet
bonnie	pretty
brae	hillside beside a river
burn	a rivulet or stream
Coila	sometimes spelled Kyla, referring to the area of Scotland called Kyle. She is a goddess of the land celebrated in Burns' poem "The Vision".
cotter	a farmer who rents his land from a landlord
dine	dinner-time
elf-candles	magical lights lit by elves
fiere	comrade
fit	foot, footstep
glen	valley
gowans	daisies
guid-willie-waught	cordial drink, goodwill drink
kelpies	water-demons
Muse	a goddess of inspiration
pint-stowp	tankard ("Surely you'll be your pint-stowp,/ And surely I'll be mine" means "we'll drink heartily together")